JAMES

PERCY

THOMAS THE TANK ENGINE BUZZ BOOKS

1   Thomas in Trouble
2   Toby and the Stout Gentleman
3   Percy Runs Away
4   Thomas and the Breakdown Train
5   Edward, Gordon and Henry
6   Thomas goes Fishing
7   Thomas down the Mine
8   James and the Troublesome Trucks
9   Gordon off the Rails
10 Thomas and Terence
11 James and the Tar Wagons
12 Thomas and Bertie
13 Thomas and the Trucks
14 Thomas's Christmas Party
15 Thomas, Percy and the Coal
16 Saved from Scrap
17 Thomas and Trevor
18 Duck Takes Charge

First published 1991 by Buzz Books,
an imprint of the Octopus Publishing Group,
Michelin House, 81 Fulham Road, London SW3 6RB

LONDON MELBOURNE AUCKLAND

ISBN 1 85591 118 3

Printed and bound in Great Britain by BPCC Hazell Books, Paulton and Aylesbury

SAVED FROM
SCRAP

buzz books

The Fat Controller works his engines hard but they are always very proud when he calls them Really Useful.

"I'm going to the scrapyard today,"
Edward called to Thomas.

"What, already? You're not that old!"
replied Thomas cheekily.

The scrapyard is full of rusty old cars and machinery. They are brought to the yard to be broken into pieces and loaded into trucks.

8

Then Edward pulls them to the steel works where they are melted down and used again.

One day, when Edward arrived in the yard, there was a surprise waiting for him. It was a traction engine.

"Hello," said Edward. "You're not broken and rusty. What are you doing here?"

"I'm Trevor," said the Traction Engine sadly. "They're going to break me up next week."

"What a shame!" said Edward.

"My driver says I only need some paint, polish and oil to be as good as new," Trevor went on sadly, "but my master says that I'm old-fashioned."

Edward snorted. "People say that *I'm* old–fashioned, but I don't care. The Fat Controller says that I'm a Useful Engine. What work did you do?" he asked.

"My master used to send us from farm to farm. We threshed corn, hauled logs and did lots of other work. We made friends at all the farms. The children loved to see us."

Trevor shut his eyes – remembering.
"Oh yes," he said. "I like children."

Edward set off for the station. "Broken up, what a shame! Broken up, what a shame!" he clanked as he went back to work. "I must help Trevor, I *must*."

He thought of all his friends who liked engines but strangely none of them would have room for a traction engine at home!

"It's a shame! It's a shame!" Edward hissed as he went over the viaduct.

Then he brought his coaches to the station.

"Peep, peep!" he whistled. "Why didn't I think of him before?"

There, on the platform, was the very person.

"Hello, Edward, you look upset," said the man. "What's the matter, Charlie?" he asked the driver.

"There's a traction engine in the scrapyard, Vicar: he'll be broken up next week.

Jem Cole says that he never drove a better engine."

"Do save him, sir. He saws wood and gives children rides," said Edward.

"We'll see," replied the Vicar.

Jem Cole came on Saturday. "The Reverend is coming to see you, Trevor. Maybe he'll buy you."

"Do you think he will?" asked Trevor hopefully.

"He will when I've lit your fire and cleaned you up," said Jem.

The Vicar and his two boys arrived that evening. Trevor hadn't felt so happy for months. He chuffered happily about the yard.

"Show your paces, Trevor," said the Vicar.

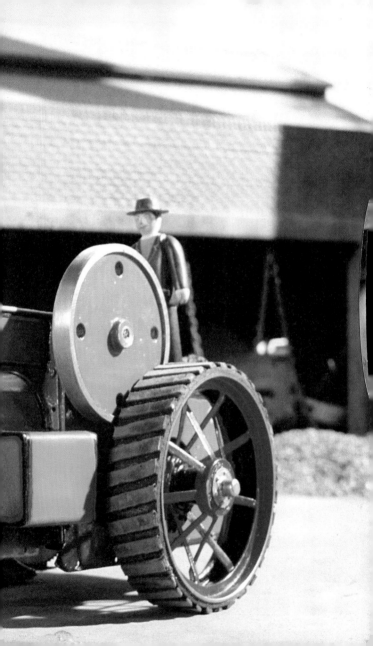

Later, the Vicar came out of the office smiling. "I've got him cheap, Jem, cheap." Jem was very pleased and ran to tell Trevor the good news.

"Do you hear that, Trevor?" cried Jem. "The Reverend's saved you and you'll live at the vicarage now."

"Peep, peep!" whistled Trevor, happily.

Now Trevor's home is in the vicarage orchard and he sees Edward every day.
His paint is spotless and his brass shines like gold.

Trevor likes his work, but his happiest day is the Church Fête.

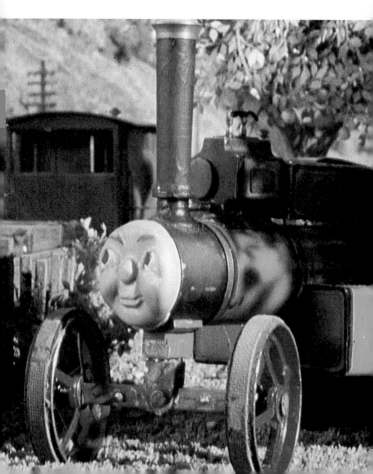

Then, with a wooden seat bolted to his bunker, he chuffers round the orchard giving rides to children.

Long afterwards you will see him shut his eyes – remembering. "I like children," he whispers happily.

THOMAS

EDWARD

GORDON